word
Play
ABC

Written and
Illustrated by

Heather
Cahoon

Walker and Company
New York

First published in the United States of America in 1999 by Walker Publishing Company, Inc.

Published simultaneously in Canada by Thomas Allen & Son Canada, Limited, Markham, Ontario

Library of Congress Cataloging-in-Publication Data
Cahoon, Heather.
Word play ABC / Written and illustrated by Heather Cahoon.
p.   cm
Summary: An illustrated alphabet book using puns and wordplay.
ISBN 0-8027-8683-9H
—ISBN 0-8027-8684-7R (reinforced)
1. English language—Alphabet—Juvenile literature.
[1. Alphabet. 2. Play on words.] I. Title.
PE1155.C34   1999
428.1—dc21   98-39614
CIP
AC

Book design by Sophie Ye Chin

Printed in Hong Kong

2 4 6 8 10 9 7 5 3 1

For
Dad
Mom
Lisa
jessie
Pat
Patrick

hello

airmail

Aa

bare feet

Bb

Crock-Pot

Cc

dragonfly

Dd

eerie

Ee

flying saucer

Ff

goose bumps

bump!

bump!

bump!

bump!

Gg

Home Sweet Home

Hh

ice cap

Ii

jaywalk

Jj

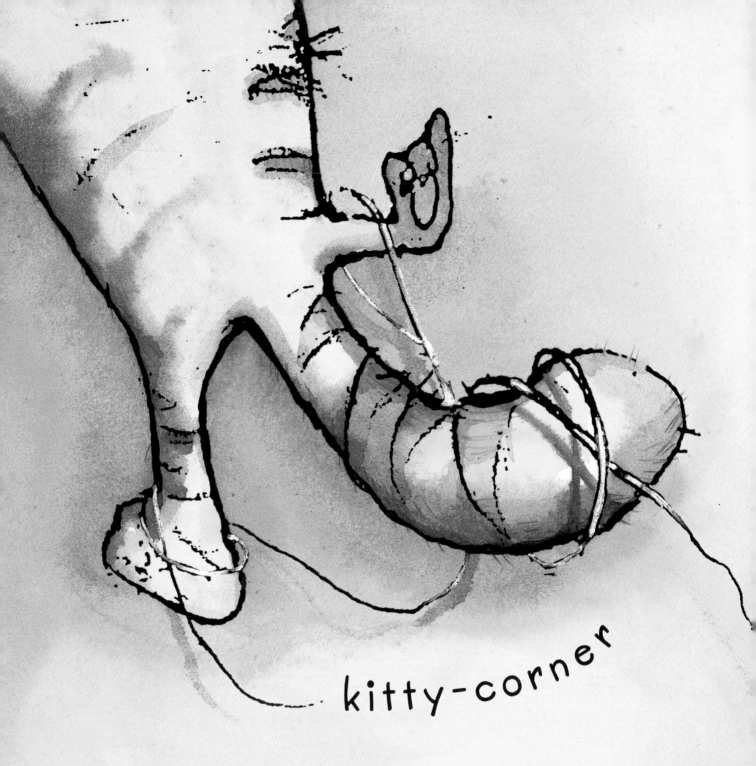

kitty-corner

Kk

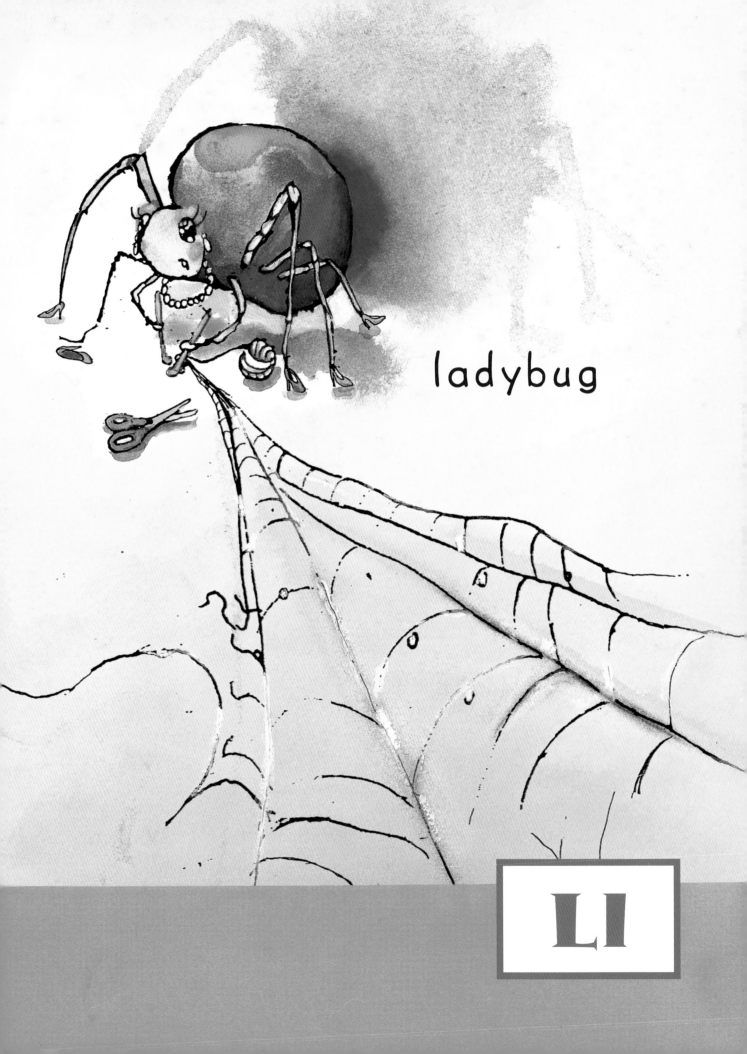

ladybug

LI

music box

Mm

night-light

Nn

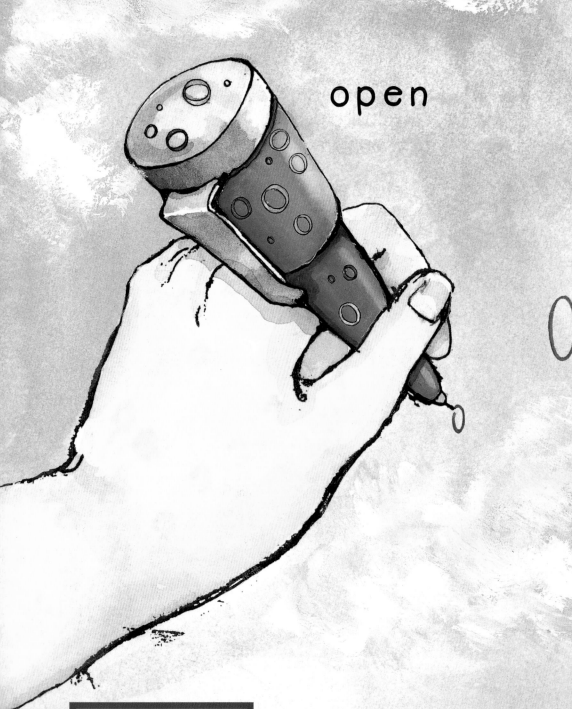

open

Oo

pantry

Pp

quarter horse

Qq

ringtoss

Rr

sunflower

Ss

teacup

Tt

undercover

Uu

viewpoint

Vv

weeping willow

Ww

yellow jacket

Yy

zippy
zip
P

Zz

airmail: a letter or package that is delivered by airplane.

bare feet: feet that aren't wearing socks or shoes.

Crock-Pot: a trademark name for a slow-cooking electric pot.

dragonfly: a very fast, harmless bug with two pairs of wings.

eerie: anything that is strange or weird enough to make a person afraid.

flying saucer: a UFO, or unidentified flying object. Many people think flying saucers are spaceships flown by aliens from outer space.

goose bumps: tiny bumps that form on the skin when a person is cold, afraid, or excited.

Home Sweet Home: what people call their home when they think it is the best place to be.

ice cap: a very large and permanent covering of ice and snow.

jaywalk: to cross a street carelessly, without paying attention to traffic rules.

kitty-corner: to be at a diagonal; also known as catty-corner.

ladybug: a small beetle with a round, spotted shell. Ladybugs help gardeners by eating harmful insects.

music box: a box that plays music.

night-light: a small light that is left on throughout the night.

open: not shut, locked, or covered.

pantry: a room or closet used for storing food, dishes, and other kitchen items.

quarter horse: a strong horse that is often used for pleasure riding and herding cattle.

ringtoss: a game where a person tries to toss rings onto a stick. This game is usually played outside during warm weather.

sunflower: a large yellow flower with a brown center. Sunflowers turn to face the sun and can grow very, very tall.

teacup: a cup used for drinking tea, a drink made from special dried tea leaves and boiling water. Tea comes from shrubs that are commonly grown in Japan, India, and China.

undercover: to do something in secret.

viewpoint: the special way each person thinks about something.

weeping willow: a tree with thin, drooping branches.

XOXO: a short, special way of writing hugs and kisses.

yellow jacket: a wasp with yellow and black markings.

zippy: to be quick and full of energy.

If you need help with the true definition of a word in this book, look it up in this

glossary.

Self-portrait

About the Author

Heather Cahoon grew up in Minnesota, where she spent a lot of time playing in the snow, sledding, ice-skating, sculpting homemade clay, and, of course, drawing. She drew colorful crayon pictures of curly haired princesses and portraits of her family. For each drawing, she had a special explanation. Heather's mom recorded these narratives and saved them for Heather to read when she learned how—so Heather was creating stories before she could write her name! (Heather's mom didn't save all of Heather's artwork. The crayon people and houses Heather drew on her pale yellow bedroom wall and on the wood staircase were soon cleaned away. . . .)

Heather no longer draws with crayons, and she now knows that drawing on walls isn't always a good idea. Heather has grown up, and her crayon-filled ice-cream bucket in Minnesota has been replaced by watercolors and computers that she uses for her work as a graphic designer in New York City. She began creating *Word Play ABC*, her picture-book debut, during summer vacation, after her second year of college.